NIGHT OF THE BLACK DRAGON

A RIDERS OF JADE AND FIRE PREQUEL

MELANIE ANSLEY

WRITING
ROOSTER
MEDIA

Copyright © 2023 by Melanie Ansley

All rights reserved.

Sign up for the author's reader list at www.melanieansley.com to receive free books, exclusives, and giveaways.

No part of this book may be reproduced in any form or by any electronic or mechanical means, including information storage and retrieval systems, without express written permission from the author, except for the use of brief quotations in a book review.

This book is a work of fiction. Characters, names, locations, events and incidents described are products of the author's imagination. Any resemblance to actual events, locations, events, or persons, living or dead, is purely coincidental.

Cover Design: Get Covers

For Evander.

CHAPTER 1

Fireworks shrieked overhead, popping in blooms of green, gold, and scarlet.

Jin tried not to stare. Doing so would only draw attention to herself and the broad-shouldered man at her side.

"How much do you think they cost?" Lu asked.

"Nothing to a wealthy couple like us."

Lu's face creased in a smile. His smooth skin and fleshy cheeks worked well for this job; he looked every bit the well-fed noble he was meant to be. He had grown out his beard into the latest style, rather than cropped short as he usually preferred it, though he gave no sign of it making him itchy or hot. Jin, on the other hand, tried to hide her discomfort in the layers of silks and the low-cut bodice she barely filled. Not to mention the sheer shawl around her shoulders and the silk shoes—flat with no grip and curled at the end. She hated wearing anything but her usual boots.

She noticed the assessing looks the other women gave her as they moved through the mansion grounds. But when they recognized neither her nor Lu, they immediately turned elsewhere, not bothering with inferiors. Good. Let her and Lu be invisible. They had chosen their clothes well—rich enough to be part of a nobleman's celebrations, but not rich enough to attract those looking to climb the heights of society.

They threaded between the guests, all with coiffed hair in gleaming black loops and gowns of every fine weave. Jin's own gown was admirably well tailored, and her hair, several shades away from black, had been piled in two great coils on her head, with three false ivory and jade combs holding it all in place. No outfit or hairstyle could overcome her hazel eyes and light skin, though. One look at her revealed her partly *huren*, or foreigner, ancestry. Ancestry that involved western, possibly barbaric, tribes. Which ones, she didn't know. She likely never would, for she knew nothing of her parents. The only physical clue she had to her origins was the tiny brand behind her left ear, in the character for "kway": precious.

"Don't fret," Lu reassured her. "You look the part."

She held her sandalwood fan up to hide her scowl. Ladies didn't scowl in public, but she knew she scowled often. "Let's find the mark and be done."

"Always in such a hurry," Lu chided. "Nothing wrong with enjoying the feast first."

They strolled with other guests into the manor's outer gardens, every detail flaunting the owner's high status. With a sprawling set of courtyards, fine walls of desert brick and gleaming tiles imported from the capital, this was a blend of Tang and Turkish aesthetic. Richly dressed servants stood at every moon gate, attentive to the guests' needs, while miniature gardens of expensive flowers burst from delicate ceramic pots lining the walkways. The air was thick with the aromas of jasmine, exotic perfume, and the famed heady wines of the region, while music from local and foreign musicians drifted from the feasting hall.

Jin inhaled, her stomach growling, but knew that none of the delicacies on offer would pass their lips. Their boss, Haitao, seemed able to smell the food in one's belly or the wine on one's tongue. The man had a sixth sense when it came to his crew indulging, and he would not hesitate to lash them if he suspected they had sampled even a single pastry ball. He believed his thieves should eat only what was necessary, and become good friends with deprivation.

Jin still bore the physical effects of days on end where she was forced to go without food. Her body was slight, and would never achieve the plump roundness that was a Han hallmark of beauty. Her face was slim, and her height small, which might have been due to her bloodline, or due to the stringent deprivations Haitao insisted on for his most trusted thieves. But Haitao had always praised her slight frame, calling her his mouse: she could get into all the places the larger rats and foxes couldn't touch. Being small had also meant she had to learn to defend herself early: small women were seen as easy targets, and she had had to pick up martial arts skills from a young age in order to fight off the bullies of the streets who would try to take her pickings, or scare her away from choice pick-pocketing spots.

They passed another moon gate into the heart of the mansion, a series of open-air courtyards festooned in bright red and black banners, each embroidered with the outline of a flying dragon. Here, guests flowed past double-storied buildings on either side and toward the main hall, marked by ornately carved wooden doors and countless silk lanterns on the eaves. A group of well-dressed noblemen stood near the entrance, surrounding a lanky man in his sixties with a long beard peppered gray and white, his rich green robes and marigold sash drawing Jin's eye. Yellow was a color saved for the imperial family, and only those in the empire's service were allowed to wear similar colors such as orange. This lanky man must be the Viceroy Chu himself.

Drums sounded, and cries of excitement rippled through the crowd as two dragons appeared over the mansion courtyards. In the lantern light, one appeared pewter and the other was dappled gold, their riders small black and tan figures sitting astride them.

Jin watched, awed but wary, as the dragons circled. Their grace and power was a stark reminder that she was just an insignificant street rat, struggling to survive in the slums of society. The dragons of the Tang empire, and the Dragon Class they belonged to, were the cornerstones of the empire's power. Jin didn't follow politics—as Haitao said, why bother with the stars when you can barely understand what's happening on the ground?—but she knew her basic history: dragons had emerged from Nine Claw Mountain to help the first Tang emperor end the Five Kingdoms War and unite the fighting regions. Since then, the dragon riders kept law and order, both within the empire and without, for almost all the bordering vassal states now accepted Tang sovereignty.

The drumbeats rose in a crescendo, and the dragons released twin lines of bright flame into the air before descending out of sight into some unknown part of the mansion. The guests clapped and shouted their appreciation, and music filled the air once again.

Tonight, Jin knew, these elites would feast, and feast well. The dragons and their riders were here to celebrate Viceroy Chu's second son, who had just graduated to the Dragon Class.

Jin tried to spot the youth who had achieved such a prestigious rank. A group of young men lounged near the balustrades of the upper balcony. Was the son the swarthy one? Even a rich man's son might turn tanned after years in the Dragon Class. But no, now she saw him—a young man, around her age of twenty years, who bore the same look and stance as his father. He was dressed in what Jin guessed must be official dragon rider leathers: a black silk vest that went to the knees, soft leather pants with a tightly woven horsehair vest, and boots shone to a high polish. What would it be like to be part of a family where the first-born was Viceroy, and the second son was now in the Dragon Class? What was it like to ride a dragon?

"You're not even listening," Lu whispered. "I see marks to the far right and near the bamboo pavilion. You?"

She snapped her fan closed and lay it across her palm, using the tip to point toward a fish pond by the banquet hall, where a group of noble ladies stood with cups of wine, laughing.

"That lady there," she said, indicating one who had just bowed her head, no doubt to show off her fine headpiece of gold and teak. "Her bracelet is white jade."

Lu cast her an admiring look. "Good eyes. Your huren blood, no doubt."

"You just can't see beyond a pretty face," she said, which made him chuckle. He liked to tease her about her mixed blood, and he was the only one who could do so without receiving a fist to the face. While huren were welcomed, mixed children like her were viewed with more hesitation in the upper class. Mixed children were the results of unsanctified marriages, as most great families chose ethnically Han brides.

She noticed he wasn't moving toward the women. "What are you waiting for?"

"Patience, noble lady," he murmured. "I sense tonight's a lucky night. There is so much on offer. Why go for a hare when we could land a deer, am I right?"

She tried to curb her impatience. Lu was setting his sights higher and higher of late, trying to steal ever more expensive items.

"This is about buying your freedom, isn't it?"

"What if it is?"

"What will you do? After you're free?"

"Open a wine house. Where all the guests are rich like these folks at the feast, and will spend money like its water," he said.

She snickered. "You won't rob them?"

He laughed back. "Only occasionally."

"Maybe I'll rob them."

His look turned serious, as if he sensed what lay unspoken in those words. "If we find something valuable enough, we might buy your freedom as well."

She made a sound of disbelief. "You're more suited to slinging wine than I am. I would end up in fights."

"You could do other things," he insisted. "Maybe protect me from thieves. Perhaps you'd like to care for the horses."

For a moment she luxuriated in the thought. A life with enough to eat and a place to sleep, where Lu only expected her to care for the customers' horses. Animals were simple to please and asked no questions. They didn't judge her by her size, her gender, or the color of her eyes. That would be a good life. But a life completely out of her reach.

"Haitao will be overjoyed with a white jade bracelet. Let's be satisfied with that and go home."

"Wait. Look."

She followed his gaze. The lanky man she assumed was Viceroy Chu had drawn out a pipe and was lighting it. She could see why Lu had paused. The pipe was in the shape of a long black dragon and, even from this distance, clearly of fine make.

"That pipe is worth much more than the bracelet," he whispered back. "That's likely black pearl, and I'll swear the eyes are ruby."

"That's the Viceroy Chu," she said from behind her fan. "Are you out of your mind?"

She had grown up living by Haitao's rules: never rob government officials.

"He's retired, remember?" Lu countered. "Not officially government."

Jin frowned. "Play with fire, perish by fire."

"With your help, it'll be easy."

His flattery landed on deaf ears. She dug her fingers in his arm, and was gratified to feel him wince. "I don't mean lifting the pipe from him. I mean the consequences after."

Lu put his hand over hers on his arm, as if to steady her. "It's just a pipe. We're not robbing his treasury. Besides, when will he next have a feast for the whole province, right here in his house?"

Before she could counter, Lu was away, having slipped her hand off his arm. She cursed under her breath. The die was cast: she had to help him or leave him. It would be smarter to leave him, but she knew she wouldn't.

She trailed him toward the staircase, keeping an eye on both Lu and the Viceroy while scanning for bodyguards. It seemed that the Viceroy had the entries and exits to his home guarded, but left the interiors relatively unpoliced. Few would wish the old Viceroy Chu bodily harm, as he was well liked and had a reputation for fairness. Only Lu was bold enough to try and rob the man himself, at his own party. Lu and now, by association, Jin.

Jin moved around a group of guests to gain a clearer view of the pipe. Lu was right: it was easily more expensive than any of the jewelry they had seen that night. Jin was sure it was worth more than she could steal in a year.

Lu was also right about one other thing, a fact that Haitao milked as often as he could: a party was the perfect time to free the wealthy of their treasures. Everyone wanted to show up looking their best, so would bring prized heirlooms and expensive finery out to flaunt before their peers, each trying to outdo the others. Drink would dull the perceptions, and no one expected to be robbed at the Viceroy's.

Haitao had drilled them repeatedly: take only one item, and no more, no matter what you see on offer. The sole item missing would simply be tallied as a random loss, the result of a careless night of drinking. Multiple items would lead to rumors of theft, and an inquiry, and more guards at future elite parties. But they had never robbed a government official. *Ex*-government official, Jin reminded herself, then cursed under her breath. She was already adopting Lu's logic to justify what they were about to do.

She gathered her flowing dress and moved up the staircase, the Viceroy's voice now audible. From the corner of her eye she could see Lu striking up a conversation with one of the men surrounding the Viceroy. Lu was no doubt using one of his favorite ploys, something about the listener being a distant relative. Viceroy Chu would be finishing his pipe soon, judging by its dwindling smoke. Sure enough, Chu took a last puff, knocked the tobacco remnants into the bowl held by a waiting servant, then tucked the pipe into a pouch at his belt.

It was time to strike.

CHAPTER 2

*J*in saw Lu tug his beard, a signal that he was about to step into place. Jin readied to insert herself when the Viceroy's attention would be averted, but then she stopped, having caught sight of another servant gliding between the guests. He walked directly up to offer the Viceroy and his friends a platter of lychee fruit, turning his back to Jin, but not before she saw his face.

Jin shot Lu a look. He too had recognized the newcomer.

They had crossed the man only a few times before, but they knew who he worked for. And it was not the Viceroy's household, despite his impeccable Chu household clothes. No, this man worked for the Iron Hawks.

Don't do it, Jin said silently. Lu wouldn't be foolish enough to pluck the pipe now, would he? But the thought of a rival getting the spoils they had chosen for themselves was clearly too much for Lu to bear. He strode

10

forward and grasped the servant's hand, inches from the pouch containing the pipe.

"This is fine silk for a servant's robe," Lu said, holding the man's arm as if to examine the weave of the material. "I must purchase something similar for my staff."

The Viceroy turned to Lu, surprised by this interruption, while the servant seemed to wrestle his fury. Only a tightening in the jaw betrayed his emotions.

"I'm sure one of my wives will tell you where they obtained it," Chu said, polite but dismissive. He and his friends deftly moved away from Lu, Jin and the false servant, indicating their company was not wanted.

"I'll have a lychee, thank you," Lu said, plucking a handful from the platter. The man's eyes narrowed.

"The city of Gaozho is clearly getting small," the servant said, icy.

"You're free to leave anytime," Lu replied.

The man glanced at Chu, then gave Lu a hateful look before melting into the crowd.

"That's the fourth time in as many months," Lu sighed when he was out of sight.

But the first time we've picked the same target, Jin thought.

Jin scanned the room. There didn't appear to be any others who might be working with him. "Let's finish this and go home." She nodded toward the koi pond in the center of the courtyard. "The lady with the bracelet is still here. And now drunk by the looks of it."

Lu looked at her in surprise. "You'd have me give up the pipe?"

Jin glared at him. "We don't need a pipe. We need

something that will keep Haitao happy and not create a city-wide war. That lady's bracelet will do nicely."

Lu swallowed the last of the lychees he had taken. "You don't dream big enough. You lack ambition."

"You lack foresight."

"Quite the opposite. This is all about foresight. What happens when you are too old to pick pockets or run away from the authorities?"

Jin hadn't thought much about growing old, because the possibility seemed unlikely. They were more likely to be knifed by a rival thief, or fall from a wall while escaping from a job.

"What if you're injured and Haitao has no use for you?" Lu asked softly. "If you break a leg or can't run, or lose your fingers to some guard dog, what do you think he'll do then?"

Jin wanted to protest that Haitao would likely find a doctor to heal them, and give them the time off they needed as they were his prized thieves. But deep down she knew that was simply what she wanted to think of the man who had saved her from starvation. If Haitao decided they were permanently lamed, or could never earn him another *fei*, he would kick them out. And depending on how he felt on the day, that might mean making sure they could never talk about what they knew of the Red Crows. There were only two ways out of Haitao's Red Crows: death, or buy-out.

"Even if you can pay back everything Haitao says he's invested in you," she said, "how do you know he'll honor his promise?" Jin had seen how Lu clung to this hope, day after day.

"He will."

"No one's bought their way out of the Red Crows, Lu. Not even that cocky teen a few years back, and he brought in more than a governor's fortune."

Lu shrugged. "He didn't ask as nicely as I will."

"Since when has being nice ever swayed Haitao?"

Worry flitted across Lu's face, and for a moment Jin regretted pricking a hole in his hopes. But she had to be realistic. Lu would get himself killed if she didn't speak some reason to him.

"He'll say yes," Lu insisted. "And if he doesn't…" He let the thought trail off, unwilling to voice anything that could be interpreted as disloyal.

Jin didn't push it. She knew Lu well enough to know what he meant. If he wasn't given his freedom, he would escape. The thought weighed heavily on her.

He seemed to sense her unease, for his expression softened.

"It'll be good with you gone." She cut him off before he could say something meant to be comforting. "More food for the rest of us, you know." She didn't want his pity.

Lu started to reply, but then swore under his breath and strode off, pulling Jin with him. She saw what had startled Lu: Chu had left his group, and was weaving through fawning guests toward a gate that led to the back of the mansions. She saw a flash of black and ruby from the pipe pouch, swinging from Chu's belt.

They followed at a discreet distance, watching him walk through another courtyard with an ornate double door at the other end. They stood and observed from afar as Chu took out a key from his pocket, unlocked a large padlock, and stepped through the double doors before closing them behind him.

"He has to come out," Lu said. "We'll lift it then."

She wanted to protest, but she could tell he had his mind set on this. She weighed the risks. It should be a simple task to get close to Chu, and take the pipe then. A week of listening to Lu griping about an opportunity lost would be more painful.

"But then we leave."

"Of course."

"Oath?"

Lu gave her an impatient look. "You're touchy today." He squeezed her arm. "Here he comes! Go!"

She barely had a chance to straighten her shawl before Chu was striding across the courtyard toward them. Lu walked off, his back to her. She discreetly pulled a comb from her hair and kept it in her palm. She waited until the official was alongside them, then deftly tossed the comb. She heard the satisfying crunch of shattered wood, and let out a cry.

Chu stopped, looking down at his feet. Jin fell to her knees next to him, picking up the broken pieces.

"My lady, I am sorry. Was this yours?"

She nodded, cradling the hairpiece in her hands. "Yes, I'm so clumsy. It must have fallen earlier..."

"I will see that my household buys you a new comb," Chu said, and awkwardly reached out a hand. She took it and stood.

"No, no, don't trouble yourself," she insisted. "It was my fault."

He bowed. "If you change your mind, please find me. This is my house and my word will be followed."

She bowed more deeply. "You are too kind, Master Chu."

He inclined his head, then moved on. When he had disappeared into the outer courtyard, Lu was upon her in an instant.

"Well?"

"It wasn't on him," Jin replied, tossing her broken comb into a potted kumquat tree next to them.

Lu cursed. "Other pocket?"

"I checked that one too."

"The Iron Hawk bastard lifted it first."

Jin shook her head. "I don't see how. He must have left it in there." She indicated the shut doors Chu had come from. A part of her was relieved. Lu had been growing ever more bold, even before today, and she was worried it would land them in the tea chambers sooner rather than later. And very few returned from "drinking tea" with the police. "We can't do the same trick twice. It's time we find another target."

"I can get us past that door."

She made a dismissive noise. "Then he'll know it was stolen. Why do you insist on one horse when there's an entire stable to choose from? I think we've spooked him. He's decided to put the pipe somewhere safe."

Lu grinned. "Even better."

"You gave me your oath we'd leave after that."

Lu held up one hand. "I promised we'd leave once we lifted the pipe. No pipe, no leaving."

A part of her wanted to punch him for his obstinacy, but part of her also admired his determination. Before she could dissuade him, Lu was off through the courtyard and working on the padlock. The man was an expert at picking locks. Jin had learned the basics, but she was nowhere near as proficient as Lu. Soon she heard a low whistle. Lu was grinning and holding the door open for her.

She checked to make sure the few guests in the courtyard were not observing them, before striding across the paving stones and stepping in. Lu followed and shut the doors, leaving the padlock hanging from the door handles on the outside.

They found themselves in a large study, with a writing desk and chair against one side and a staircase leading to the second floor on the other. Scrolls lay piled neatly in the center of the desk, with an ornate ink stone and brush stand to the side. Shelves of books covered the walls, and an imposing cabinet stood in the corner.

Lu immediately headed toward it, while Jin went to the desk. Lu probed every inch of the cabinet, clearly sure he would find it there, but she had a feeling he was wasting his time. Men of letters were proud of their ability, of their education and their many hours memorizing the Confucian teachings. They were likely to keep things of value near those things, if only out of some subconscious association: education was precious, therefore precious things would be kept near objects of education.

Inside the first drawer lay writing supplies, neatly written notes, and bound papers, but nothing of real value. She pushed it closed carefully, then moved to the second. This time luck favored her: inside lay the pouch she'd seen at Chu's belt. She pulled the pouch up and felt the satisfying weight, then upended the bag and let the dragon pipe fall into her hand.

"Lu."

Lu let out a crow of victory, having looked up and seen her standing with the pipe. "Well done!" He came and admired it. "It's a beauty, and will fetch a high price."

A high price meant it would save them a beating from Haitao. It had been a while since she'd returned with a displeasing haul, but she had the scars to remind her of what happened when she aborted a job, or mistook a wood comb for teak.

She tucked the pipe, pouch and all, into a secure fold in her sash. Lu went to the door and was about to open it when he spun around and gestured at Jin.

Someone was coming. And there was no time to get out.

CHAPTER 3

*J*in dropped to the floor and rolled under a nearby *kang* daybed, sucking her belly to her spine and crushing her voluminous dress to her. Lu darted behind a curtain partition, drawing his dagger from his belt. Jin's mouth went dry. A street brawl was one thing—she had survived more than she could count. Drawing blood from a noble, however, would be a first. A first she didn't care to try.

The sound of voices reached them, then the door swung open. Jin could see boots, but nothing more. One set was stout and gleaming: the Viceroy's. The other set was mud-spattered and worn with journeying, but well made and military by the cut of them.

She heard the door close, then the Viceroy said, "But I received no notice, General."

"You're receiving notice now." The other voice sounded younger, but more authoritative. "They will be here in a week's time. Perhaps less."

The Viceroy's boots padded to his desk, where he sat

down. Jin prayed he wouldn't open anything. She winced when she heard the scrape of a drawer, a rustle of paper, and a brush. But then the drawer shut again, and there were no exclamations of surprise.

"What are you doing?"

"Writing this down," the Viceroy replied. "I must instruct my son—"

"You'll write nothing down," the younger voice said, sharp. "We'd like to keep this as discreet as possible. And there's a good reason why I am seeking the help of the father and not the son."

For a younger man to speak that way to his elder was unthinkable. The General clearly held a very powerful rank.

There was a surprised pause, then the sound of papers being pushed aside and brushes put down. "Of course, General. This unworthy servant is at your service."

Jin wondered if Lu was as tense as she was. She worried that her dress would slip from her fingers and poke out the side, and already one of her elaborate hairpins had caught in the underside of the kang. She tried to dislodge it by turning her head.

"…Red Crows in the area."

Jin froze. She made her heart slow long enough to hear the Viceroy's reply.

"That's greatly exaggerated. We have control of every highway here."

"I need the truth, Viceroy Chu."

"This humble servant is no longer Viceroy, General."

"But the empress believes you might have…experience, shall we say, that your son might not. You will be rewarded for truth. What are the safest roads through the province?"

So the General had heard of Haitao's Red Crows, and their attacks on the main highways through the province of Kwannay. Haitao ran a very proficient operation, one that maintained good intelligence on every road and inn, where rich merchants flowed in regular convoys across the Silk Road. True, the Crows had grown more daring in recent months because of the intensifying competition with the Iron Hawks, but Haitao paid a decent bribe to keep the lower-ranking officials pliant. And though Viceroy Chu had made a fair attempt to stamp out Haitao and his clan, Chu's son and successor was less interested in securing the highways and more interested in his family's coffers. That made him an ideal Viceroy for Haitao's purposes. Viceroy Chu's son had a reputation that had traveled far, and this conversation would be embarrassing for the Viceroy.

The Viceroy cleared his throat. "I'd avoid the main ones. But there are no inns large enough to accommodate the Dragon Class on most of the lesser roads. I recommend an inn by the river town Kuanghe. It's run by a distant relative of mine, and I can count on him to be discreet."

The floorboards creaked as the guest paced to the other side of the room. "Its name?"

"The Golden Horse. It's at the crossroads of the Eastern highway between Gaochang and the road from Yingzho."

"I will pass that name to the Dragon Class guards.

Please inform your relative. We cannot risk our cargo, for it is beyond priceless."

"This humble servant understands, General. You have my word that we will make sure it is well protected."

"Good. They will be passing through in a week's time —ten days at most if things get delayed. Paperwork and such. The Empire appreciates your help in the matter."

To Jin's ear, his tone implied that help was expected, not appreciated. The Viceroy gave a quick murmur of agreement before the General made his obligatory farewells and departed. The Viceroy followed him out, and she heard the click of the padlock from the outside.

The lock!

It was impossible to lock a padlock behind oneself, and they had planned to get out the same way. The Viceroy must have been distracted enough by his conversation with the General not to have noticed it was open when he arrived.

Now, they were stuck inside the study, locked in from outside with no obvious way of escape.

CHAPTER 4

Jin pulled herself from underneath the *kang*, snapping her hairpiece. She shoved the two halves into her sash with the pipe. She was running out of hairpieces.

Lu had emerged from where he'd been hiding behind the partition, and headed to the windows.

She held little hope, but went to the nearest one and cracked the shutter open. As she suspected, the window was a lattice of finely carved wood, designed to allow airflow but to keep birds—and people—from entering the study.

"Upstairs." Lu led the way up, emerging into a sitting room with several *kangs* along the walls. Four balcony doors faced the east, and these opened easily when Jin pulled on them. They stepped out and peered cautiously over the balustrade.

Below them spread a garden full of guests, servants weaving through with offerings of wine, apricots, and sweetened taro. They couldn't climb out this way unseen.

Lu motioned her over to another balcony on the south side.

Jin peered out and saw a sloping roof that ended in a small courtyard. This area appeared closed to guests, with barred doors on the opposite wall. A copse of towering bamboo hid what lay beyond the wall, but they didn't have much choice.

"You have the pipe?" Lu asked. Jin nodded. Lu nimbly hopped out the window and onto the roof tiles, took a few experimental steps, and held out a hand to Jin. But she clambered out by herself, unwilling to hold onto him. Despite her cumbersome skirts, she was still better at balancing. Besides, if she were to fall, she'd rather not take Lu with her. His considerable bulk landing on her would crush her bones, if not kill her outright. They balanced along the edge and made their careful way toward the curved ridges at the end of the roof, where carved dragons warded off evil spirits. Lu crouched and gripped the edge, then swung himself over and down, cursing as he sliced his hand on the tile. She dropped next to him in the courtyard.

"It's just a scratch, baby brother."

He grunted his annoyance. At seven years her senior, she could almost call him uncle. He quickly bandaged his wound with a kerchief from his pocket before he could bleed over the courtyard stones.

She unbarred the one door that led in the opposite direction of the party. They hurried through it, into a long open-air corridor with moonlit gardens and ponds on either side. Four round gates led to different areas of the mansion. Jin hurried to follow Lu through the one on the right.

Here, however, she paused, sensing a change in the air. It smelled not just of smoke, but of sulfur, and something else she couldn't pinpoint.

Jin looked over toward the smell, and froze. A giant wedge-shaped head, blacker than the shadows around it, rested its chin on the far wall. Ridges rose around its skull like a crown of bone, and she could see the glint of eyes. In the dark, she couldn't gauge its exact size, but the head itself was larger than her entire body. The beast opened its jaws, revealing teeth that were each as long as Jin's forearm. For the first time that night, Jin felt jagged, naked fear.

A dragon.

They had somehow found their way to the dragons' stable. Jin was looking death in the face.

CHAPTER 5

Before she could shout a warning to Lu, a blast of warm air pummeled her, flooding her nose with the smell of wood ash and smoke. She crouched into a defense stance, her blade out of her sash and in her hand, where it looked laughably small against the great dragon's bulk.

Just as Jin prepared for the dragon to snap her up or engulf her with flame, a shout sounded, and a burst of light lit the sky.

The beast before her rose against the moon. In the glow of the fireworks, she could see its wingspan was at least five times her body length, and it had an elegant tapered head and ridges all along its back. The Viceroy's second son rode on its back, gripping the dragon's leather reins in one hand as he soared into the sky.

Jin stared. She had never seen a dragon so close before. The Kuannay prefecture had always been a remote post; besides occasional passes of dragons overhead on their way from the capital to the furthest borders during unrest, the inhabitants here never saw dragons up close the way some of the other provinces did.

The creature made a musical trumpeting sound, like the blowing of some great pipe. Cheers rose from the courtyards underneath it. The dragon landed on one of the tiled roofs, like some giant cat, expertly balanced despite its huge bulk.

"Jin, come!"

Lu's sharp voice drew her back. Lu had managed to open one of the courtyard doors, and Jin forced herself to stand and take a steadying breath. She needed to look her part more than ever, not like a thief scared about being seen by a dragon. She and Lu strolled casually, like guests who had lost their way, through the rest of the manor.

Her heart thudded erratically, but this didn't upset her so much as the inexplicable envy she had felt upon seeing the dragon. She had been in danger of being outed, possibly arrested then and there. Yet, for a crazy moment, the dragon's sheer grace and power had made Jin wish that she could sit astride one, if only once. But dragons were like happiness: the purview of the wealthy, not for street rats. What would she do with a dragon? Why was she wasting time even asking such a question?

They found a wall and scaled it to the other side, landing safely in the common streets with its familiar smells: smoldering wood stoves and cheap wine, tossed out food slop and horse dung. Her heart began its usual rhythm again, soothed by the comforts of the familiar.

She fell into step with Lu. "Haitao will be happy. The pipe is a fine one," she said, touching the prize in her sash. Her thoughts tugged back to the black dragon perched on the roof. She knew little about dragons, but she had heard they had keen eyes, and an even keener sense of smell. Could it have seen them? Unlikely; they would have been captured already. "But I don't care to rob a house with a dragon again."

When Lu didn't answer, she glanced at him. He seemed lost in thought.

"Lu? Where's your head? I thought you'd be drunk with happiness."

He looked at her, as if just remembering she was there. "Forget the pipe, Jin. Did you not hear a word in there?"

She frowned. "The talk of cargo? Even Haitao wouldn't be so stupid." At his look she sighed. "We rob barons and rich merchants. That General was from the imperial court. Whatever they are transporting must be valuable, but you'd be mad to rob an imperial convoy."

Lu refused to be deterred. "The General said it was priceless. If a General earning that much thinks it's priceless, then it's beyond even Haitao's dreams. And Haitao believes in taking risks when the time is right."

"It's never the right time to lose your head." Haitao's mantra came out of her almost automatically, which grated on her. She wasn't a coward; she simply had enough healthy fear to keep her alive. She had not survived being orphaned, rescued by one of the more notorious thieves in the empire, and trained into an expert thief herself without knowing when to be bold and when to fold, as Haitao often said. That did not make her the same as Haitao. Did it? "If it's treason, it's beheading."

Lu grunted, stepping around a pile of camel excrement. "That's overly dramatic. Stealing's not treason."

"If it's stealing from the empire, it might be."

Lu didn't answer, and Jin sighed in exasperation. "I know you want to buy your freedom, but what if it's just not possible?"

"It's our only hope, Jin." Lu looked wistful. "I know you don't remember a life before this, but Haitao took me when I was seven. I have memories."

Jin scowled again, though not with malice. She had heard Lu talk of his family before, of a simple but loving home, where his parents ran an ink shop in the calligraphy quarter. It hadn't been a rich life, she was sure, but from their present situation it sounded like heaven. Loving parents, meals that didn't come only when you had picked enough pockets or made a large heist that day. And unlike Jin, Lu hadn't been saved from the streets. When his parents died in the fire that took all their worldly possessions, his uncle had sold him to Haitao rather than add an extra mouth at his table.

"Life can be different, Jin." Lu's voice hardened. "It SHOULD be different. I want to have that life back. I want to show you a life that's worth living."

Jin felt a burst of exasperation. "What if I'm grateful for what I have, Lu? What if it'll never be different for me? Stop filling me with these dreams that will never be. Haitao is the closest thing to a father I have, and this is the best I can hope for. Let's take the pipe back and be done."

Lu fell silent.

They continued southwest, away from the wealthier neighborhoods and into the denser market areas. As they neared the towering Green Cloud pagoda that marked

Gaozho's city center, Lu turned down a side street lined with closed shutters.

This street was neutral territory, the dividing line between the thief clans. As a lone woman picking pockets, Jin usually avoided it out of extreme caution.

"It's quicker," Lu said, seeing her hesitation. "We'll make it back in half the time."

They passed several other couples, many stumbling through the streets and giggling with the effects of wine. Jin supposed her askew hair, torn dress, and *huren* eyes made her fit in. There were plenty of mixed-race singing girls and courtesans in the city, and the patrolling night watchman clearly took her for one of those, heading home with a client.

She stiffened as they passed. Growing up, she had always had to defend herself from the men in the thieving clans. She had few fears—Haitao had made sure of that. But one fear she had never been able to shake was that of being sold to a singing house. She had always preferred the illegal activity of stealing to the legal activity of being a courtesan. She would rather take a thousand beatings from Haitao than suffer the fates of those women.

"Don't worry. If Haitao threatens to sell you to a song house, I'll volunteer to take your place," Lu said with a straight face.

She almost laughed, then a thin figure materialized out of the shadows, his knife flicking the light from a nearby teahouse lantern. Lu and Jin slowed, then stopped when they saw the man's face.

"Looks like we both tired of the party." The servant's clothes were gone, replaced by a loose tunic and hat that could have been worn by any tradesman in the city. Jin and Lu turned to retrace their steps, but a burly man with a topknot and thick beard had blocked their retreat.

"I believe you have something of mine," the first thief said. He pulled up his sleeves, revealing a telltale feather tattoo on his inside arm. Whereas the Iron Hawk leader demanded all his thieves mark themselves as a sign of loyalty, Haitao derided the practice. A thief must blend in, not stand out, Haitao believed. A tattoo was useful only for getting thieves identified and caught, which led to the tea rooms.

"Iron Hawks and Red Crows have a truce," Jin said. "We have a right to be in the shared streets."

The man examined her more closely, as if surprised she would speak back to him.

"You stole from me. Give it back, or I lose my manners."

"We lifted it first, honorable sirs," Lu said. "By my reasoning, it's ours. All's fair in thieving, isn't it?"

"The one who has the knife decides what's fair," the Iron Hawk answered. "And I say I saw the pipe first."

"Really, sirs, I took the Iron Hawks to be better losers than this. If you can't lose gracefully, don't play the game," Lu said.

The Iron Hawk's expression turned ugly, and he nodded toward Lu's bandage. "It looks like you might not be at your best today. Why don't you sit down like a good dog, and find another bone to chew."

Lu bridled at the insult, and one fist clenched.

Jin heard the man behind them shift on his feet, getting ready to attack. They were treading very dangerous territory now, with few options open. Giving up their prize would mean a severe punishment from Haitao. Fighting might spark something worse.

"We don't want a clan war, brothers," Jin said.

The Iron Hawk looked her over in a way that chilled her blood. "You're very talkative for a girl. You must be the little sparrow they say Haitao keeps. And perhaps beds?" He grinned at her reaction. "What will you offer to keep the peace, girl?"

The man reached out to take her arm. Without a second thought, Jin's dagger was free, and in the next instant it was buried in the man's shoulder, hilt deep. The Iron Hawk looked down, surprised, before Jin pulled it out. Then she felt herself picked up from behind and thrown against a door. Her head sparked in pain, and something scraped her bare shoulder, but she was back on her feet in a heartbeat. Lu had delivered a kick to the Iron Hawk's head, knocking him to the ground, while the giant burly one advanced on Jin. She swept up the dagger from where it had fallen next to her, focused past the stars swimming in her vision, and threw. The blade found the giant's throat, bringing the man to his knees and then face-down into the street.

She stood for a moment, panting. Lu took in the devastation, looking shaken for the first time that night.

"What were you thinking?" Lu hissed. "Couldn't you have gone for the leg?"

She walked over to the giant and began trying to turn him over. "Help me. I can't leave my blade here."

Lu dutifully shoved at the huge body, and they retrieved her dagger from the corpse's throat. Blood flecked Jin's dress, but the pipe was still safely in her sash.

Lu nodded toward the wiry man, still unconscious in the street. "You'd better finish him off so he can't tell the Iron Hawks."

Jin shook her head.

Lu gave her a hard look. "This is not one of Haitao's exercises, Jin. We kill him, no one's the wiser, and we avoid a clan war."

"I'm a thief, not a murderer." Killing an attacker bent on hurting her was one thing. But she couldn't bring herself to kill someone who was already down.

Lu shook his head. "And you say I'm the one with no foresight." He drew a dagger from his sash and advanced. Jin was about to stop him when a scream erupted from above them.

They looked up at the second-story window of the teahouse. A woman was pointing at them and shouting loud enough to wake the whole district. "Thieves! Help! Police!"

Jin grabbed Lu by the arm. "Leave him, we have to go!" If they were seen killing the man, there would definitely be no mercy if they landed in the police tea rooms.

Lu cursed, but leapt up after her. They ran through the rest of the alley in silence and back to Red Crow turf. A clan war was now inevitable. Jin didn't want to think what the price would be.

CHAPTER 6

Haitao and his inner crew of twelve changed headquarters every new moon, so as to stay hidden and thwart any spies that might betray them to the authorities, or to the Iron Hawks. Haitao had as many connections as a spider had webs, and had an endless array of tea shops, wine houses, and shopkeepers who allowed him and his team to stay.

They stood for a moment in front of the entry to their latest headquarters, a nondescript dried goods warehouse in the traders' district. Neither relished the prospect of explaining things to their boss.

"I'll do the talking, remember," Lu said. There was no reproach in it, simply the unspoken promise to defend her no matter what. Jin nodded, her throat tight.

Lu rapped on the door with their signature knock, and the usual hired hand, a stick-thin boy, opened the door and let them slip in. They walked into a narrow courtyard with a gnarled pine twisting up through the center, then into the back rooms.

Even at this late hour, Haitao was waiting up for them, a few lanterns spilling warm light in the corner. Haitao liked to keep his rooms sparsely furnished, with just a few choice items to remind him of his rule over thievery in the western province. He was thickset and jowly, with a surprisingly lush beard for a Han man, and brooding eyebrows. But many made the fatal mistake of assuming his bulk was fat. He was anything but. He had arms that could still wield a club without effort, and he was quick on his feet despite those feet being attached to short legs and a midsection like a barrel. He was reading a letter by the lantern light, but looked up expectantly and put it aside at their entry.

"Greetings, Master Haitao," Lu said, as he and Jin knelt, then bowed low to the floor.

Though Haitao referred to himself as their father, he insisted on formalities. Familiarity, in his view, bred contempt, and he often quoted the sage Confucius' teachings to remind them that filial piety underpinned everything in life.

Haitao crossed his arms, taking in their blood-spattered clothes. "What happened?"

Jin reached into her sash and pulled out the pipe. It felt as beautiful as it looked. In the drab surroundings of Haitao's room, it seemed even more exquisite. A phoenix among hens. She handed it over, though she had little hope that this would soften the bad news they had to share.

Haitao examined every detail, from the ruby eyes to the ivory teeth. Jin could see the greed in his face, before he tamped it down and put the item aside. "A fine piece. Though the blood on you tells me things didn't go smoothly."

"It was my fault, Master Haitao," Lu said. "I suggested we take the shared roads to get the pipe back sooner, and we ran into two men. Iron Hawks. They attacked us."

Jin didn't react outwardly, but her heart thudded. Lu was trying to protect her. Haitao had taught her, brutally at times, to love no one, but Lu was perhaps the closest she could come to truly caring about someone.

"Why would they attack you on shared roads, when that is forbidden?"

"They were also at Viceroy Chu's, Master Haitao." Lu kept his face to the ground. "They had wanted the pipe themselves, and were upset that we'd taken it."

"Any deaths?" Haitao's voice was quiet.

"One."

A silence fell. Then came a rustle of clothing as Haitao stood. Jin could sense the anger building. The air crackled with it.

"You son of a dog. Do you know what you've done?"

There was no defense, Jin knew. Even though they had been attacked, it had been on shared turf. Blood was not to be spilled on shared turf.

"Master Haitao," Jin ventured, "perhaps we could offer the pipe to them."

Haitao's slap, when it came, cracked hard against her face. She stayed on her knees, however, refusing to fall.

"I thought I taught you to not be naïve!" he hissed. "This is bloodshed, girl. Not some drunken insult!" Haitao leaned over her, his voice murderous. "I just might give you over to them, if I thought they'd take your skinny carcass."

Jin's gut twisted, but she stayed silent.

"Master Haitao, perhaps this is an omen."

Jin chanced a look over at Lu, confused. He didn't meet her gaze, instead keeping his eyes on the floor.

"What nonsense are you peddling?" Haitao snapped.

"The truce with the Iron Hawks has always been inconvenient," Lu said. "And the city is getting too small for both clans to work without conflict. What if this is a chance to wipe out the Iron Hawks?"

"What?" Haitao smirked. "Did you steal Viceroy Chu's army along with his pipe?"

*Don't do it...*but even as Jin thought it, Lu was already speaking.

"We found out about a priceless cargo passing through the Western Regions in the next few days."

"What kind of cargo?"

"Something of great value—so much so that an imperial General was personally asking Viceroy Chu to make sure it had safe passage and avoided the Red Crows' territory."

Haitao sat back down in his chair. "And how will this wipe out the Iron Hawks?"

"We heard them mention the inn that the convoy will stop at, Master Haitao." Lu paused for effect. "And when. We could rob it."

Haitao snorted. "Are you trying to get every soldier hunting us down, along with the Iron Hawks?"

"They won't be hunting us down if it's the Iron Hawks who stole the cargo."

Another long silence fell. Jin's mind raced. Though bold, Lu's proposal wasn't entirely without merit. The audacity to steal from the Dragon Class itself would definitely bring the wrath of Viceroy Chu and the entire empire down on the culprits, wiping them out. The trick was to make sure they thought the culprits were the Iron Hawks.

Haitao's eyes narrowed. "Tell me exactly what you heard. And how."

By the time Lu had finished recounting the conversation from the study, Jin could see that Haitao was sorely tested. The temptation of such a coup was unparalleled—an imperial convoy that held a priceless cargo, and the chance to eradicate his nemesis as well. But of course, such a venture carried eye-watering risks.

Haitao stood, and began a slow measured pace of the room. Lu let him pace. He and Jin both knew this meant that the seed of the idea was taking root. Jin felt torn, sensing the next moment might decide all their fates. Lu darted her a look, as if to say, *this is our chance. Don't ruin it.*

"Jin," Haitao said. "What do you think the cargo is? You heard nothing of what it might be?"

"Just that it's headed to the north. They want to keep it discreet."

Haitao grunted in such a way that she knew this intrigued him even more.

"If it's military," Lu added, "it's likely gifts for another state or province. Worth a fortune."

"You're suggesting robbing from the heart of government. You know my rules, Lu."

"Of course, Master Haitao," Lu agreed. "And wise rules for normal times. But as the wise sage Confucius said, the gods cannot help those who refuse opportunity when it presents itself."

The sly fox. Jin could sense Haitao shifting.

"You agree, Wang Kway Jin?"

He only used her full name when he wanted her to agree to something he couldn't decide on. He was tempted, and wanted others to back the decision. Though he could switch from kindness to cruelty in a heartbeat, she knew that, in a twisted way, Haitao valued her opinion, because her fate was tied to his.

The die was cast. The only way out now was to rip the Iron Hawks out by their roots.

"I agree. If it's priceless but meant for a lesser lord, we could possibly overtake it, and make sure that the Dragon Class sees us wearing Iron Hawk tattoos."

Haitao nodded. "I'll ask my sources to find out what's inside. In the meantime, I'll try to hold off the Iron Hawks." He shook his head. "They'll be frothing at the mouth. But," and here he gave them a wicked smile. "If we go ahead with the robbery, I want you two to lead it. If anything goes wrong, it will be you two sitting down for tea, you understand."

Jin's heart thudded, but Lu seemed relieved. He nodded. "You can count on us, Master Haitao. We won't let you down." He stood, head still bowed low. "And of course, we will be entitled to our share of the cut when it's done?"

Master Haitao looked at Lu shrewdly, as if assessing. "Yes. You'll get your twenty percent."

"Thank you, Master Haitao. I would like to use it to buy my freedom, with your blessing."

Haitao snorted. "If you're alive at the end of this escapade, you can choose to forfeit your twenty percent for your freedom."

Lu looked up. "That is kind, Master Haitao. And usual for a usual raid. However, this would be wiping out the Iron Hawks entirely. Surely you can spare me part of my cut, as I cannot leave the Red Crows with empty pockets."

"I'll take fifteen percent as your buy-out price. You may have five percent for your future. My last offer," Haitao said.

"Yes, Master Haitao."

Jin could almost taste the anticipation in Lu, the surge of joy. She felt happy for him, that he could have this hope to solve all his problems in one fell swoop. For a moment she felt it rub off on her. Maybe Lu was right. Maybe there was a way out of this life of thievery and fear, though she could scarcely imagine it.

"Now go," Haitao said. "Get cook to make you something to eat and then sleep. We'll need to move quickly, while keeping the Iron Hawks from killing us first."

Lu and Jin left him, and went to the kitchens to scrounge a quick bowl of noodles with vegetables and a few slices of salted pork. Haitao never let them gorge, even after a difficult and successful run, and his cooks knew this.

Lu slurped his noodles loudly, while Jin ate slowly and silently, trying to savor her food and make it last. This cook was quite good, and made a decent broth. It would sustain her past breakfast, if Haitao decided to get them up early and make them skip their morning meal.

"You're happy," she said, when Lu had finished his bowl and licked his chopsticks clean.

"Of course. I'd rather risk everything than be stuck here, Jin." He gestured around them. "What's so great about all this?"

She swallowed the last of her broth. "We're alive."

Lu shook his head. "Alive is not the same as living. You heard Master Haitao, Jin. Ask him for the same deal. Exchange your cut for a new life. You know I'd always welcome you."

His words needled her. Lu could afford such thoughts, but not her. Not a girl from the street who had nowhere to go and no skills outside of thieving and fighting. "I'll help you rob the Dragon Class convoy. And I hope you buy your freedom. But…I can't come with you."

"Why not?"

"I just can't."

"You don't believe it will work."

"I don't believe Haitao would let me go."

"And you're worried that if you say you want to go, he'll punish you for being ungrateful."

She said nothing, but they both knew it was true. Lu leaving was understandable, as he had been bought. But Haitao would view Jin leaving as a deep betrayal. She knew she would miss Lu, but she couldn't go with him.

He stood and came beside her, placing a hand on her shoulder. "This job will be a good thing, you'll see."

"Let's hope so," she said. "If it goes wrong, we'll either have our throats slit by the Iron Hawks, or be sitting down to tea with the imperial police." She paused, frowning. "What do you think the cargo is, anyway?"

"A carriage full of gold and jade."

"Or maybe the lost treasure of Bandit Pangli."

"Fine horses from the Sogdian empire?"

"Let's hope not," she replied, appalled. A herd of horses would be a headache to steal. "If the Buddha smiles on us, it'll be something small but priceless."

It was Lu's turn to be dry. "And when does the Buddha ever smile on thieves?"

They bantered without pause as they readied themselves for bed, fantasizing about the riches that awaited them.

As Jin slept, however, it wasn't the thought of gold or silver that filled her dreams. Instead, she kept seeing a dragon rising over the mansion, its wings eclipsing the moon. Only instead of being black, this dragon was a deep rich green, like the finest of jades. And instead of the Viceroy's second son, the rider crouched against the dragon's neck was Jin.

She had robbed a Viceroy, and now she would rob the Dragon Class. She would wipe out the Iron Hawks, so that Haitao could run the city like a king, and she could be his right hand. Everything would fall into place.

Meanwhile, thousands of *li* away in the heart of the empire's capital, the cargo that would seal Jin's and the empire's fate was being carefully packed into an ornate box. Special attendants in uniforms bearing the crest of the Dragon Class were gingerly loading the box onto an imperial transport carrier, and specially selected riders were saddling their fleet of dragons to transport this priceless cargo to its destination. A destination they would never see.

Next in series: "Dragon Class". Order today through your favourite bookstore, or via the author's website: www.melanieansley.com

AUTHOR'S NOTE

Thanks for reading "Night of the Black Dragon"! This story came about because I grew up in China most of my life, and my first language was Chinese. I speak both Mandarin and Cantonese, and have always been fascinated by Tang China because it was considered a golden age. It was a time of relative tolerance, and the capital was a mixing pot of cultures from all over China as well as what's now called the Middle East and Central Asia. I like to think that because of this, many people like Jin and me —half Chinese and half "huren"—existed.

When writing historical fiction, even historical fantasy, readers are understandably curious where fact ends and fiction begins. I've used the Tang dynasty circa AD 700 to 750 as an inspiration for this story world, and tried to remain true to certain details like modes of dress, foods, and prevalent religions. However, I've also taken huge liberties with details such as systems of spelling, certain party and banquet customs, how long Empress Wu was in power, not to mention the presence of dragons! I hope you enjoyed this story for its entertainment value and the world it creates. But I wouldn't recommend it for passing any exams on Chinese history.

Still have questions? I'd love to answer them if I can! Please feel free to contact me at melanie (at) melanie ansley (dot) com.

And I hope you'll join Jin on her next heist in the first book of the "Riders of Jade and Fire" series, which will be coming soon! You can subscribe to my readers group to be first to know about its release later this year, simply sign up at my website: www.melanieansley.com.

ACKNOWLEDGMENTS

Every book, long or short, takes multiple people to bring it to life, and *Night of the Black Dragon* is no different.

Thanks to Sam for always being my alpha reader and story ninja. Thanks to my beta readers and also to my editor, Nick Hodgson, for polishing this and pointing out my redundancies.

Thank you to the ARC team: Kelley, Johnette, Jerry, Edward, Mindy, Lynette, Prenscella, Vicky, Ina, Cecilia, Renee, Sandra, Calvin, Valynda, Susan, Vanessa, Krystina, Jonathan, and Kendra. Without you all I wouldn't have a great group to champion the release. Thank you for taking time to read this story before everyone else.

Last but not least, thanks to all the readers and Facebook followers who have come along with me on this journey. I appreciate each one of you!

Thanks for reading! If you enjoyed this, why not join my reader list? You'll be first to know all the news on Jin's adventures in the *Riders of Jade and Fire* series, plus you'll receive:

* *The Queen and the Dagger*, the prequel to the *Book of Theo* fantasy adventure series;

* exclusive previews, giveaways, and bonus stories. JOIN NOW at www.melanieansley.com

If you enjoyed *Night of the Black Dragon*, please consider leaving a review on Amazon and Goodreads. You'll be ensuring many more of Jin's adventures follow.

<u>Praise for "Dragon Class":</u>
"You don't want to miss this one!"
"Couldn't put this book down!"
"Anyone who loves 'Fourth Wing', this is the book for you!"

Melanie was born in Canada but raised in China, and now lives in Ballarat, Australia with her husband and two children. She loves to read, write, and laugh. She also makes movies.